only the adoration of listeners and viewers but a host of prestigious awards, including a record-breaking six Emmy awards—two of them for his greatest achievement, *The Twilight Zone*.

The worlds and characters presented over the course of five seasons, beginning in October 1959, were like nothing audiences had seen before. Television, the new "must have" appliance for America's increasingly prosperous households, offered comedies such as *I Love Lucy* and *The Honeymooners*, news programs including Edward R. Murrow's *See It Now*, as well as Westerns, game shows, and soap operas. With a typewriter as his spade, Serling dug beneath the surface of the expected and planted the seeds of a more imaginative and thoughtful genre, writing more than half of the show's 156 episodes while producing and hosting all of them. He bravely took on themes of oppression, prejudice, and paranoia, all the while giving people what they needed at the end of the day: entertainment.

While he had his run-ins with censorship, Serling's clever use of other worlds and veiled scenarios generally protected him. As he explained, what he couldn't have a Republican or a Democrat espouse on the show, he could have an alien profess without offending the sponsors. This approach also allowed viewers to take away whatever message best suited them; the more reflective could consider the psychological and political implications, while others might be satisfied with simply enjoying the thrill of the surface story. So much more than mere science fiction or fantasy, Serling's scripts are parables that explore the multifaceted natures of hope, fear, humanity, loneliness, and self-delusion.

Half a century later, *The Twilight Zone* remains a part of our culture, routinely referenced in print and on television, having become a shorthand expression that succinctly describes the bizarre and unexpected. The original episodes are still aired on the SciFi Channel, both in late-night slots and as day-long marathons. The show was literally a Who's Who of Hollywood, helping to foster the careers of fledgling actors including Robert Redford, Ron Howard, Dennis Hopper, Charles Bronson, and William Shatner. It has also inspired countless authors and filmmakers, who have gone on to break through boundaries of their own.

In the fifty years since *The Twilight Zone* first aired, we've faced new enemies and have altered our definitions of happiness, but our core hopes and fears remain the same, as does our desire to be entertained. The stories are as compelling, and as telling, as ever. And now, in their newest incarnation, Serling's scripts serve as the basis for this graphic novel series, which honors the original text and even echoes the storyboarding of television, but offers a fresh interpretation, as seen through the eyes of a new generation of artists.

—Anna Marlis Burgard
Director of Industry Partnerships, Savannah College of Art and Design

You're traveling through
another dimension,
a dimension not only of sight and sound
but of mind;
a journey into a wondrous land
whose boundaries
are that of imagination.
That's the signpost up ahead—
your next stop,
the Twilight Zone!

BINGLE BINGLE BINGLE biiing . . .

THIS IS MAPLE STREET ON A LATE SATURDAY AFTERNOON.

MAPLE STREET IN THE LAST CALM AND REFLECTIVE MOMENT...

SHhhhhRRRRRR

...BEFORE THE MONSTERS COME!

RRRSHHHRUMMMRRMM

I'LL CUT ACROSS THE BACKYARD . . .

. . . SEE IF THEY GOT POWER OVER ON FLORAL STREET.

AYBE SOME KIND OF ELECTRICAL STORM.

DOESN'T MAKE SENSE. WHY SHOULD EVERYTHING SHUT DOWN LIKE THIS?

NAH. NO LIGHTNING. NO THUNDER. NO NOTHING.

WHY DON'T WE GO DOWNTOWN AND CHECK WITH THE POLICE?

OVER A LITTLE POWER FAILURE? THEY'LL THINK YOU'RE NUTS.

IT ISN'T JUST A POWER FAILURE, DON. IF IT WERE, WE'D STILL BE ABLE TO GET SOMETHING ON THE RADIO.

THAT'S RIGHT . . .

I DON'T LIKE THIS . . .

MY RADIO DOESN'T WORK EITHER . . .

WE'RE CUT OFF . . .

AWFULLY DARK OUT THERE . . .

SOMEONE SHOULD GO SEE WHAT'S GOING ON . . .

I'LL TAKE A RUN DOWNTOWN. MAYBE I CAN GET IT STRAIGHTENED OUT.

CLICK CLICK

IT WAS WORKING FINE BEFORE—

WHAT DOES IT MEAN?

MAYBE WE'D BETTER **WALK** DOWNTOWN.

THAT'S THE CAUSE OF THE POWER FAILURE . . .

. . . AND ALL THE REST OF IT.

METEORS CAN DO CRAZY THINGS . . .

. . . LIKE SUNSPOTS.

SURE. SURE. SUNSPOTS RAISE CAIN WITH RADIO RECEPTION ALL OVER THE WORLD. THIS THING BEING SO CLOSE— THERE'S NO TELLING THE SORT OF STUFF IT CAN DO.

MR. BRAND! PLEASE DON'T LEAVE.

LEMME GO!

YOU MIGHT NOT EVEN BE ABLE TO GET TO TOWN.

THEY WERE WAITING OUT IN THE DARK. IT WAS THAT WAY IN THE MOVIES. NOBODY COULD LEAVE.

NOBODY EXCEPT—

EXCEPT WHO?

EXCEPT THE PEOPLE THEY'D SENT DOWN AHEAD, THE ONES THAT LOOKED HUMAN.

AND IT WASN'T UNTIL THE SHIP LANDED THAT—

TOMMY! PLEASE, SON, . . . DON'T TALK LIKE THAT.

THAT WAS THE WAY THEY PREPARED THINGS FOR THEIR INVASION.

THEY SENT FOUR PEOPLE. A MOTHER AND A FATHER AND TWO KIDS WHO LOOKED JUST LIKE HUMANS . . . BUT THEY WEREN'T!

WELL, I GUESS WHAT WE NEED TO DO IS TO RUN A CHECK OF THE NEIGHBORHOOD AND FIND OUT WHICH ONES OF US ARE REALLY HUMAN.

CRAZIEST THING I EVER HEARD...

KID TELLS US A COMIC BOOK PLOT, AND WE STAND HERE LISTENING!

NO USE STANDING AROUND MAKING BUM JOKES. ANYBODY KNOW WHAT'S THE DEAL OVER ON FLORAL STREET? PETE VAN HORN BACK...

...YET?

Ha Ha Ha

heh heh heh

RrRrRr Rr

RrRrRr

Rr-Rr-Rr

rr click click

DOES YOUR CAR START, LES?

NOPE.

NOTHING SEEMS TO BE WORKING. CAN'T EVEN GET THE CAR—

RRRRR
VROOOM!

IT . . . STARTED!

VROOO

VROOM!

VROOOM!

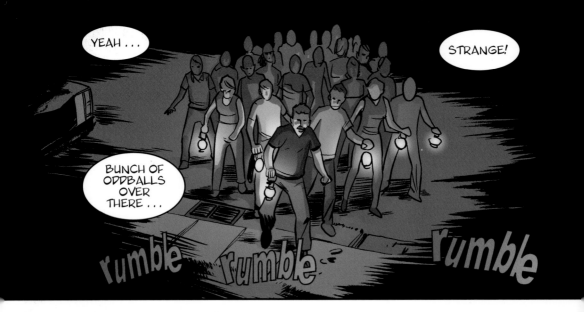

WE'RE . . .

WE'RE ON A MONSTER KICK, LES.

SEEMS THE GENERAL IMPRESSION NOW HOLDS THAT MAYBE THERE'S A FAMILY THAT . . . ISN'T WHAT WE THINK IT IS . . .

. . . MONSTERS FROM OUTER SPACE OR SOMETHING. DIFFERENT FROM US.

FIFTH COLUMNISTS FROM THE VAST BEYOND.

NOW DO YOU KNOW ANYBODY WHO MIGHT FIT THAT DESCRIPTION AROUND HERE ON MAPLE STREET?

WHAT IS THIS, A PRACTICAL JOKE OR SOMETHING?

RRrr—VROOM! VROO

OR YOU, CHARLIE! OR ANY OF US, IT SEEMS.

FROM AGE EIGHT ON UP!

WHAT I WANT TO KNOW IS— WHAT ARE WE GONNA DO? JUST STAND AROUND ALL NIGHT?

ONE OF 'EM'LL TIP THEIR HAND.

THEY GOT TO.

OH, THERE'S SOMETHING YOU CAN DO, CHARLIE!

YOU CAN GO INSIDE AND KEEP YOUR MOUTH SHUT. YOU CAN JUST CLIMB INTO BED AND FORGET IT.

YOU SOUND PRETTY ANXIOUS TO HAVE THAT HAPPEN, STEVE. I GUESS WE REALLY OUGHTA KEEP AN EYE ON **YOU** TOO.

YOUR WIFE'S BEEN DOING A LITTLE TALKING, AND I THINK MAYBE EVERYTHING SHOULD COME OUT NOW . . .

ABOUT SOME ODD THINGS YOU'VE BEEN DOIN'.

WHAT?!

YEAH?

GO AHEAD, DON. TELL US WHAT SHE SAID.

MYRA'S TOLD THE MISSUS ABOUT HOW THERE'S BEEN PLENTY OF NIGHTS YOU SPENT HOURS DOWN IN THE BASEMENT . . .

ORKIN' ON SOME ND OF RADIO OR METHING. WELL, NE OF US HAVE VER SEEN THAT RADIO—

WE WERE JUST TALKING OVER TEA—I DIDN'T MEAN . . .

WHAT KIND OF RADIO SET YOU WORKIN' ON? I NEVER SEEN IT. NEITHER HAS ANYONE ELSE.

WHO TALKS TO YOU ON THAT, UH . . . RADIO SET?

LET'S PICK OUT EVERY IDIOSYNCRASY OF EVERY MAN, WOMAN, AND CHILD ON THIS WHOLE STREET. NOW HOW ABOUT A FIRING SQUAD AT DAWN, CHARLIE TO GET RID OF ALL THE SUSPECTS?

NARROW THEM DOWN FOR YOU. MAKE IT EASIER. HUH?

RIGHT, DON? THAT OKAY WITH YOU?

STEVE! STEVE, PLEASE BE REASONABLE!

IT'S JUST A HAM RADIO SET. A LOT OF PEOPLE HAVE THEM. I'LL SHOW IT TO YOU.

NO! NO, WE WON'T SHOW 'EM ANYTHING.

IF THEY WANT TO LOOK INSIDE OUR HOUSE, LET THEM GET A SEARCH WARRANT.

I'M SURPRISED AT YOU, CHARLIE. HOW COME YOU'RE SO DENSE ALL OF A SUDDEN?

WHO DO I TALK TO?

WHY, I TALK TO MONSTERS FROM OUTER SPACE.

I TALK TO THREE-HEADED GREEN MEN WHO FLY OVER HERE IN WHAT LOOK LIKE METEORS.

LOOK, BUDDY . . .

. . . YOU CAN'T AFFORD TO—

YOU GOT HIM!

GIMME MY GUN BACK, STEVE!

NO! NO!

I DON'T KNOW WHY THE LIGHTS ARE ON.

NO! STOP THIS!

CRACK!

NO ONE'S EVER GONNA USE THIS GUN AGAIN!

THAT DOESN'T STOP ANYTHING, STEVE. THERE'S PLENTY MORE GUNS...

...'COURSE, WE DON'T 'SPECIALLY NEED GUNS.

SOMEBODY'S PULLING A GAG OR SOMETHING!

I DON'T KNOW WHY THE LIGHTS ARE ON. I SWEAR I DON'T!

OOOF...

IT'S THE KID, IT'S TOMMY. H-H-HE'S THE ONE!

UNG . . .

IT ISN'T SO!

THE KID **KNEW** WHAT WAS GOING TO HAPPEN!

HE WAS THE ONE WHO **KNEW!**

IT ISN'T SO. HE'S A LITTLE BOY.

THUD

STEVE!

GET THE KID!

FIRST ME, NOW THE KID, HUH, DON?

IT'S NOT GONNA GO THAT WAY!

KA-WHAM!

DON? NO... WHAT HAVE I DONE?

THE ONE! HE'S ONE! IT'S NOT HE'S THE ONE!

OH MY GOD!

WHAT ABOUT HIM! DIDN'T HE KEEP TRYING TO TELL US ALL WHAT TO DO?

GET UP, YOU! YOU HIT STEVE FIRST! GET UP, YOU ROTTEN LOUSE!

EN CHARLIE SAID SHOULD KEEP AN ON HIM! HIM AND HIS RADIO!

OU POINTING HE FINGER AT ME, LES?

I SHOULD HAVE LET THEM AT YOU!

ZZT

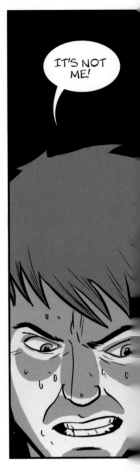

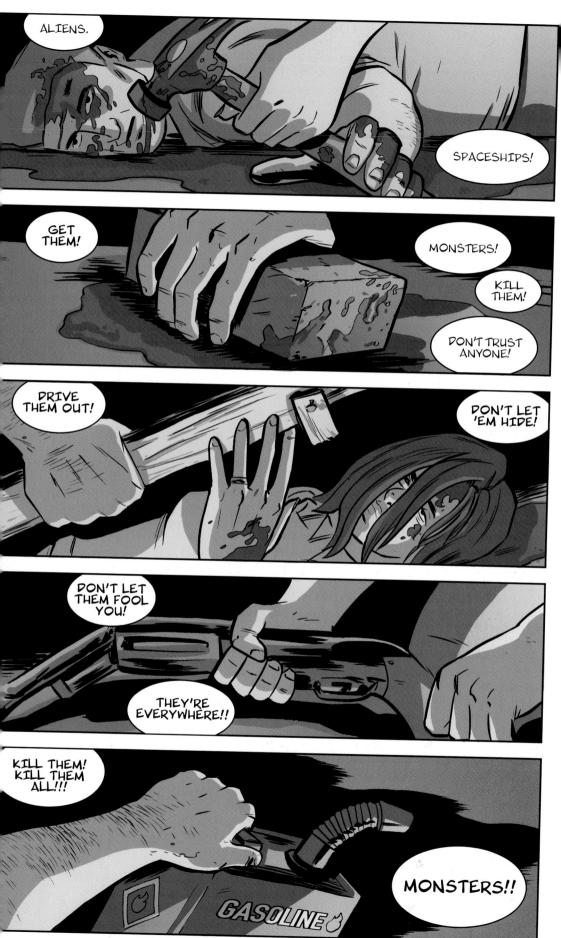

THE TOOLS OF CONQUEST DO NOT NECESSARILY COME WITH BOMBS AND EXPLOSIONS AND FALLOUT.

THERE ARE WEAPONS THAT ARE SIMPLY THOUGHTS, ATTITUDES, PREJUDICES—FOUND ONLY IN THE PETTINESS OF THE HUMAN MIND.

RRRSHHRNNNNNRRNN

FOR THE RECORD, PREJUDICES CAN KILL AND SUSPICION CAN DESTROY, AND A THOUGHTLESS, FRIGHTENED SEARCH FOR A SCAPEGOAT HAS A FALLOUT ALL ITS OWN . . . FOR THE CHILDREN . . .

. . . AND THE CHILDREN YET UNBORN.

AND THE PITY OF IT IS . . . THAT THESE THINGS CANNOT BE CONFINED . . .

. . . TO THE TWILIGHT ZONE.

The Monsters Are Due on Maple Street

Season One, Episode #22

Original Air Date: March 4, 1960

Written by Rod Serling

Cast

Narrator: Rod Serling

Steve Brand: Claude Akins*
*Also appeared in *The Little People* as Cmdr William Fletcher

Les Goodman: Barry Atwater

Charlie Farnsworth: Jack Weston*
* Also appeared in *The Bard* as Julius Moomer

Tommy: Jan Handzlik

Woman: Amzie Strickland

Don: Burt Metcalfe

Tommy's Mother: Mary Gregory*
*Also appeared in *The Shelter* as Mrs. Henderson
and *The Lateness of the Hour* as Nelda

Man: Jason Johnson*
*Also appeared in *The Lateness of the Hour* as Jensen

Mrs. Brand: Anne Barton*
*Also appeared in *Shadow Play* as Carol Ritchie

Mrs. Goodman: Leah Waggner (as Lea Waggner)

Old Woman: Joan Sudlow

Pete Van Horn: Ben Erway

Charlie's Wife: Lyn Guild

Alien: Sheldon Allman

Alien: Bill Walsh (as William Walsh)

Crew

Producer: Buck Houghton

Director: Ron Winston (as Ronald Winston)

Director of Photography: George T. Clemens

Music: René Garriguenc (as Rene Garriguenc)

Film Editor: Bill Mosher

Production Note

Science fiction buffs might find the aliens at the end of this episode a bit familiar.
The space suits and spaceship were borrowed from the movie *Forbidden Planet*.

ADAPTING STORIES FROM ROD SERLING'S
THE TWILIGHT ZONE

In terms of screenwriting adaptations it's trying to cut out stuff that's extraneous, without doing damage to the original piece, because you owe a debt of some respect to the original author.

—Rod Serling, 1975

At first, the idea sounded straightforward. Take an original *Twilight Zone* screenplay and adapt it into a graphic novel—break the visuals into panels, move the dialogue into balloons and captions. After all, Rod Serling himself was a fan of comics, and graphic novels are their visual and literary heirs. Serling collected Entertaining Comics titles such as *Tales from the Crypt* and *Weird Science*, the themes of which resonate in *The Twilight Zone*; even Serling's trademark narration could be considered an echo of the Crypt Keeper's introductions. Yet the more I considered the task of adapting the scripts, the more the gravity of what I was doing set in. I grew up watching *The Twilight Zone*, after all, as did so many Americans. The work required a certain reverential perspective, considering the show's iconic status, not to mention the quality of the original material.

In the 1950s the comics Serling had enjoyed were considered subversive, a threat to America's youth. Frederick Wertham published *Seduction of the Innocent* in 1954, excoriating comics in an atmosphere of public paranoia similar to a scene from *The Monsters Are Due on Maple Street*. A year later, a Senate committee was convened to investigate the pernicious influence of horror comics on America's youth, and the Comics Code Authority was established to censor comics' content. EC Comics went out of business as a direct result. In an interesting twist of fate, by the end of the decade *The Twilight Zone* was just beginning to find its television audience with stories that probably would not have made it past the comics censors. Recreating Serling's stories now, in graphic novel form, seems appropriate, emblematic of an era in which comics are finding a new readership, achieving new respect, and speaking to a new audience receptive to a more sophisticated message.

Serling's stories run the gamut from serious drama, filled with fantastic and frightening dilemmas of the human condition, to wry, tongue-in-cheek humor in a sci-fi wrapper. Selecting eight as graphic novel material meant making difficult choices. Serling was a prolific writer, creating more than half of *The Twilight Zone*'s 156 scripts. It was not only a question of which of these would work best in novelized format, but which ones, as a group, would come closest to capturing the essence of *The Twilight Zone*. The stories ultimately chosen for these books possess the strongest visual possibilities and reflect an effort to achieve a cross section of Serling's dramatic range.

As I began adapting the stories for artists, I immersed myself in the screenplays and watched each episode until I felt I had internalized not just the characters, the plot, and the point, but what I imagined to be something of the author himself. In the process, I felt a growing kinship with Serling. Parts of the screenplay were often deleted from the actual show. Lines, characters, even entire scenes were struck, sometimes for budgetary reasons, sometimes because of time constraints, sometimes perhaps because Serling himself may have anticipated problems with the scenes. The show usually had only a thirty-minute time slot. The deleted scenes, however, often add richness and complexity to the story, offering a glimmer into what Serling might have done were it not for the constraints of the television medium. Restoring scenes seemed to help push the story even harder. I felt as if I were developing Serling's original design, following the telling to its logical conclusion.

With each of these stories, I have aspired to take advantage of what the graphic novel format can do. Art and text draw the reader deeply into the narrative. The reader does not just hear, but ponders, actively bridging the gaps between the panels of art with his or her own imagination. The story doesn't just happen to the reader, but, in part, *is* the reader. In other words, *The Twilight Zone* episodes had to be recreated not just to fit into a graphic novel format but to belong to it.

As much as possible, I have endeavored to keep the intentions of the original story intact—that is the "debt of respect" owed to Serling—fully functional in a new medium. From some nearby fifth dimension, I hope Serling is smiling at the prospect of these books, pleased at the thought of a new generation arriving by way of a different avenue perhaps, but entering and being welcomed into the fold of "Zonies" around the world.

—Mark Kneece
Professor of Sequential Art, Savannah College of Art and Design

Our thanks go to Carol Serling for her time and consideration while reviewing the adaptation
texts and illustrated pages, and also to John Lowe, chair of the Sequential Art Department at Savannah
College of Art and Design, for his assistance in pairing the right artists with the right stories.

Bloomsbury Publishing, London, Berlin and New York

First published in Great Britain in 2009 by Bloomsbury Publishing Plc
36 Soho Square, London, W1D 3QY

First published in the USA in 2009 by Walker & Company
175 Fifth Avenue, New York, NY 10010

Packaged by Design Press, a division of Savannah College of Art and Design, Inc.®
22 East Lathrop Street, Savannah, Georgia 31415, USA

Adaptation from Rod Serling's original script by Mark Kneece
Illustrated by Rich Ellis
Inks by Robert Grabe
Lettering by Mia Paluzzi and Matthew Razzano
Series title treatment by Devin O'Bryan
Series copyediting by Kerri O'Hern
Series creative development by Anna Marlis Burgard and Emily Easton
Series art direction and design by Angela Rojas
Series project management by Angela Rojas and Melissa Kavonic
Creative consultant: Carol Serling

Photograph of Rod Serling © Bettmann/Corbis

A CIP catalogue record of this book is available from the British Library

ISBN 978 0 7475 8791 0

Printed in China by C & C Offset

1 3 5 7 9 10 8 6 4 2

www.bloomsbury.com/childrens
The Savannah College of Art and Design: www.scad.edu